THE
CHERRY PIE
PRINCESS

THE
CHERRY PIE
PRINCESS

VIVIAN FRENCH
illustrated by Marta Kissi

WALKER
BOOKS

First published 2017 by Walker Books Ltd
87 Vauxhall Walk, London SE11 5HJ

2 4 6 8 10 9 7 5 3 1

Text © 2017 Vivian French
Illustrations © 2017 Marta Długołecka

The right of Vivian French and Marta Długołecka
to be identified as author and illustrator respectively
of this work has been asserted by them in accordance
with the Copyright, Designs and Patents Act 1988

This book has been typeset in Berkeley Oldstyle Book

Printed and bound in Great Britain by Clays Ltd, St Ives plc

British Library Cataloguing in Publication Data:
a catalogue record for this book is available
from the British Library

ISBN 978-1-4063-6897-0

www.walker.co.uk

For Audrey, with much love from Gran

V.F.

For James, with all my love

M.K.

Chapter One

BONG! BONG! BONG! Bong! Bong! Bong! Bong!
Bong! Bong! The clock in Grating Public Library
struck nine, and Miss Denzil clapped her hands.
"At last! Today's the day!" She smiled at the date
on the calendar. Not only was it underlined, it
was also ringed in red, and had a wobbly gold
star attached by a pin. "Today the princesses are
coming to OUR library."

Lionel Longbeard, an elderly dwarf and the
head librarian, shook his head. "Don't get your
hopes up, Miss Denzil. They're only coming
because their governess thinks it's a good idea."

Miss Denzil stared at him. "But Mr Longbeard! Our library is wonderful!"

"Princesses don't read," Lionel Longbeard told her. "They think it's beneath them. They'll be in and out in a couple of minutes ... just you wait and see!"

Miss Denzil, who had only recently started working at the library, was shocked. "Really? Oh, dearie, dearie me. And we're not allowed to speak to them?"

"Most definitely not." Lionel Longbeard pointed to an official-looking document on his desk. It was headed "Required Behaviour During Visits From Royalty" and was written in purple ink. The opening line read, "Under NO circumstances is a member of the public permitted to address a member of the Royal Family", and was followed by a long paragraph giving details of the dungeon that had been set aside for anyone foolish enough to make a chatty remark.

Miss Denzil read the warning in silence. "Goodness!" she said as she finished. "Not very friendly, are they?"

"They don't need to be friendly," the librarian told her.

"They're the Royal Family."

"Well, I must admit I'm disappointed." Miss Denzil removed the gold star from the calendar. "How many princesses are coming?"

Lionel Longbeard inspected a second document. "Seven."

"Are they pretty?" Miss Denzil asked. "Oh, I do hope they are!"

The dwarf shrugged. "They giggle a lot."

The assistant librarian sighed and took herself off to dust a row of books.

When the princesses arrived, they were under the care of a well-upholstered governess. She marched into the library and they followed, sniggering.

"What a lot of books!" The princess who had spoken sounded disapproving. "Couldn't they think of something more interesting to put on the shelves?"

"Like pretty hats," a taller princess suggested.

"Or handbags!"

"Dear girl, you have SUCH sweet ideas!" The governess beamed at her charge.

"This is a dreadfully boring place." A third princess was pouting. "Do let's go, Miss Beef."

There was a chorus of agreement. "Boring! SO boring!"

"Of course, my dears." The governess curtsied and headed for the door. Six of the princesses swept after her, noses in the air.

One princess was left: the youngest. She came hurrying towards Lionel and Miss Denzil. "I'm so sorry about my sisters – I absolutely LOVE your library! Please tell me, where are the storybooks? And what are those big old books over there? Can anyone borrow books?" And then, leaning over the librarian's desk, her eyes wide and hopeful, she whispered, "Are there any books that tell you how to DO things? Like … like cooking?"

"Peony!" The governess was standing in the

doorway, her sharp voice echoing round the room. "Princess Peony? I trust you are NOT asking questions!"

"No, Miss Beef." The princess jumped back, smoothing her dress. "I'm just coming, Miss Beef."

She ran towards the door where the governess was tapping her foot in an irritated manner ... and Lionel Longbeard lost his head. Ignoring all the instructions on Required Behaviour, he called after her, "Yes! Yes, Princess – of course there are! LOTS of books!"

The princess's eyes lit up – and she was gone.

The librarian sank back in his chair. His heart was beating fast, and he wondered what on earth could have made him behave in such a very foolish way.

"That was really brave," Miss Denzil said admiringly, before adding, "But, oh! Mr Longbeard! Wasn't it terribly, terribly dangerous?"

*   *   *

Miss Denzil was right. Miss Beef was only too delighted to report Lionel Longbeard's shocking behaviour to the king. The king was outraged and, unknown to his daughter, gave his orders. The soldiers arrived to arrest the librarian the same afternoon; when a small and trembling pageboy came tiptoeing into the library late that evening and quavered, "Please … Princess Peony wants to borrow a book about cooking," there was only a weeping Miss Denzil to answer his request.

The book, *A Thousand Simple Recipes for Pies, Puddings and Pastries*, was not returned.

Chapter Two

THE YEARS ROLLED BY. Princess Peony and her six sisters grew older and taller, and some grew more beautiful and others did not, which made them very spiteful.

Peony wasn't bothered about such things. Her sisters took no notice of her; she was the youngest, after all, and she had her library book for company. She spent her spare time in the palace kitchen trying different recipes for pies, puddings and pastries, until one day her father, making an unexpected visit to check on his cook, found her wearing an apron and covered in flour.

"When will you learn to behave like a princess?" he roared. "The kitchen is for servants!"

"But I like cooking," Peony said. "And actually, Father, it was me who made the cherry pie for your birthday lunch. You said it was absolutely delicious and the best cherry pie you'd ever eaten." She giggled. "You gave Cook a silver sixpence. She wanted to give it to me, but I said she could keep it."

Her father went purple with rage. "YOU? You've been making PIES?"

Peony nodded. "Cherry pies are my best. It's lucky we've got an orchard with such nice cherries. My pastries aren't so successful, but Geoffrey says I'll get better with practice."

"Geoffrey? Prince Geoffrey of Newbiggin?" A faint hope could be heard in the king's voice.

"No, Father! Goodness – he couldn't tell a grape from a gooseberry. Geoffrey the cook's boy, of course."

For a long moment King Thoroughgood was speechless. It was bad enough that his daughter had been spending time in the kitchen, but to be on friendly terms with a cook's boy ... that was too much. Much too much. Geoffrey and the cook were only saved from instant dismissal by Peony's promise that she would never, ever set foot in the palace kitchen again.

*   *   *

From then on all Princess Peony could do was wander round the palace grounds, or sit in the musicians' gallery above the royal banqueting hall watching the kitchen staff bringing pies, puddings and pastries to the royal table. She noticed that there were never any cherry pies, and she sighed. *Father must have forbidden them,* she thought. *And I know they're his favourite! But I suppose they'd remind him of me.*

As the months went on, Peony found it too depressing to sit in the gallery. She made a chart for herself, and worked out exactly how many hours it was until her thirteenth birthday. Every time she crossed off another twenty-four hours, her spirits lifted a little. When the princesses reached thirteen years of age they were allowed to leave the palace on Monday afternoons for educational purposes … and Princess Peony had a very clear idea about what might constitute an educational purpose. She was going to go back to the library, and she was going to borrow another book.

Chapter Three

NOT LONG BEFORE Peony's thirteenth birthday there was a great event. A new royal baby was born – and it was a boy. King Thoroughgood and Queen Dilys were ecstatic. Barrels of weak ginger ale were sent to every village and posters were pinned on trees, inviting everyone to rejoice with the Royal Family.

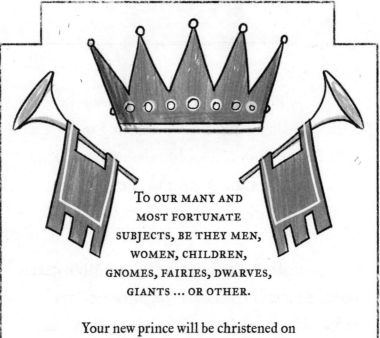

TO OUR MANY AND
MOST FORTUNATE
SUBJECTS, BE THEY MEN,
WOMEN, CHILDREN,
GNOMES, FAIRIES, DWARVES,
GIANTS ... OR OTHER.

Your new prince will be christened on
Midsummer's Morning.

All are hereby instructed to drink to Prince
Vicenzo's health, wealth and happiness.

Rejoicing will last for 30 days.

King Thoroughgood   *Queen Dilys*

P.S. All empty barrels are to be returned WITHOUT FAIL.

The Royal Christening was to be a truly glittering party.

"We will invite all the most important people in the kingdom and beyond," the king said.

"And the Fairy Godmothers," said the queen. "I believe they bring wonderful gifts."

The king looked doubtful. "What kind of gifts?"

"The usual kind of fairy gifts, dear." The queen waved a hand. "A splendid singing voice, or a never-ending supply of jokes, or a crock of gold that never runs out."

"That could be useful," the king agreed, "although I'm not so sure about the singing. And certainly not the jokes. I can't stand jokes. Had a dreadful fellow here once – wanted to be a jester, or some such thing. Had to get rid of him, of course. Gold, on the other hand, is always acceptable. Very well then – we'll invite the Fairy Godmothers. How many are there?"

"Three, I believe." Queen Dilys frowned. "And there's a rather doubtful sort of person who lives in Scrabster's Hump. She's called the Hag."

It was King Thoroughgood's turn to frown. "We don't want anyone like that. Make sure she's not invited. We only want guests of quality, Dilys. And wealth, of course. I'll be delighted to welcome the important, the grand and the wealthy."

"And I'm sure they'll be delighted to come, dear," the queen said soothingly.

Peony's six older sisters were less than delighted.

"What about us?" Azabelle demanded.

"*We* don't ever get a party!" said Bettina.

"Will we have new dresses?" Clothilde wanted to know.

"I'll only kiss that baby if Mother buys me new shoes." Donnetta folded her arms.

Emmadine scowled. "Well, I want a new dress

and new shoes before I kiss ANYTHING!"

Fabrizia ran to ask her mother and came back beaming. "We're to have new dresses AND new shoes," she reported. "And Mother says lots of handsome princes have been invited to the christening breakfast."

This news cheered the princesses, and it was decided that the new baby wasn't altogether a bad idea.

"Are we allowed to cuddle him?" Peony asked.

Azabelle snorted. "Cuddle him? Why would he want to be cuddled by you?"

"I like babies," Peony said. "And he is our little brother."

"And WE'RE his big sisters." Bettina glared at Peony. "We get to cuddle him first. You'll have to wait your turn; you'll be last."

But the older sisters never asked to cuddle the little prince. Peony tiptoed up to the royal nursery, but Miss Beef was on guard and would only allow her the merest peek at the baby. Peony just had time to see that he had flaming red hair and a button nose, and she sighed as she walked back to her room.

"I'd love to sing him songs. And tell him stories. If I could ever get back to that library I could borrow a book on knitting, and I could knit him the dearest little green jacket…"

But the baby's nurse, instructed by Miss Beef, declared he needed Peace and Quiet and No Germs until after he was christened. The next time Peony came tiptoeing to the door she was told to go away, and not to come bothering everyone again. Disappointed, she walked down to the orchard and collected several handfuls of cherries before wandering back to sit on the palace steps. There, as she sat eating her cherries, she was joined by the palace cat. The cat sat down beside her, purring.

"Hello, puss," Peony said. "I haven't seen you for quite a while."

The cat's purr grew louder,

and Peony smiled at him as they sat comfortably together in the sunshine. "I wonder where you go to when you're not here? Somewhere nice, I hope."

Miss Beef, who happened to be bustling past, sniffed loudly. "All cats are vermin," she snapped. "Riddled with fleas, without a doubt. Shoo! Shoo! Be off with you! And do NOT leave those cherry stones on the steps, Peony."

As Miss Beef went one way and the cat fled

the other way, Peony picked up the cherry stones with a sigh and put them in her pocket. "Miss Beef spoils everything," she said crossly. "She won't even let me be friends with a cat." She looked round, but there was no sign of her furry acquaintance. "And now I won't see him again for ages. I do wish he were mine..."

The cat had been in and out of the palace for years. Sometimes he was to be found in the stables, or the kitchen, or strolling through the royal apartments, and at other times he simply vanished. He occasionally allowed Peony to stroke him, but mostly he remained aloof. He particularly liked to sit in high places where he could see, but not be seen.

The youngest housemaid, who had twice found him crouched on top of Peony's wardrobe, was wary of him. "It's like he's spying on us, Miss."

Peony had laughed the idea away. "I think he's

just being a cat. What would he find to spy on here?"

But the housemaid was right: the cat was indeed a spy.

Chapter Four

THE CAT'S NAME WAS BASIL, and he was newly returned from Murk, where the Fairy Godmothers lived – a journey he made every two or three months. There he was expected to report on the latest doings of the king and the Royal Family. He had never been complimentary about any of them, with the exception of Peony.

"Peony's – how shall I put it? Different," he explained, after ending a boring account of daily events at the palace. "She's unusually kind, and she's thoughtful as well."

"Interesting." Fairy Jacqueline made a note.

"Poor child," said Fairy Geraldine. "The rest of them sound shockingly selfish."

Fairy Josephine sighed. "I've said it before, and I'll say it again: they ought to have asked us to the girls' christenings. We could have done so much for them, especially the plain ones."

"Beauty isn't everything, Josephine." Fairy Jacqueline snapped. "But you're right. We should have been asked."

That the palace had never asked the fairies for anything was the subject of much discussion and disapproval. Without practice the fairies' magical powers were withering away; even a request for the removal of a wart would have been appreciated, but no such request ever came.

Fairy Jacqueline shook her head. "I've almost forgotten how to turn rags into satins and silks."

"I practise on the kettle," Fairy Geraldine said brightly. "Last week I filled it with daisies entirely by magic!"

"So you did," Fairy Jacqueline said sourly. "And you meant it to be gold, so you can hardly count that as a success. Besides, it made the tea taste dreadful for days."

Fairy Geraldine looked sulky, and Fairy Josephine turned back to the cat. "So, friend Basil – is anything else happening at the palace?"

"Merrow!" Basil had been saving the most important item of news until the end. "Ahem. There's a new baby – and it's a boy!"

"A boy?" Fairy Josephine gave a little trill of astonishment. "Oh! Oh my goodness me – a little prince!"

Fairy Geraldine forgot to be sulky. "Surely they'll have a Royal Christening for a baby boy…"

"Really, Geraldine!" Fairy Jacqueline was disapproving. "You sound as if you think a boy is more important than a girl. To my mind, a princess has all the value of a prince."

"Of course, dear," Fairy Geraldine agreed. "But after all those girls … they're sure to be a little pleased, don't you think?"

Fairy Jacqueline sniffed. "King Thoroughgood and Queen Dilys sound exceptionally foolish, so I expect you're right. We'll see."

"We will go if we're invited, won't we?" Fairy Geraldine asked anxiously.

"Naturally." Fairy Jacqueline nodded. "But we have yet to hear if a christening is to take place."

Basil, who was cleaning his whiskers, looked

up. "Oh yes," he said. "Didn't I say? There's to be a wonderfully grand Royal Christening Breakfast. No expense spared. 'A truly glittering party', the queen said. And you're all to be invited." He stretched and jumped down to the floor. "But now I must be off. Things to do … princesses to check up on." And away he went, leaving the fairies in a state of huge excitement.

"What wonderful news!" Fairy Geraldine clapped her hands. "When the invitation arrives I shall accept at once."

"Of course," Fairy Josephine agreed. "And we must think what gifts would be suitable for the new prince. What a shame our magic isn't a little more up-to-date; a straight nose and a noble profile are so very appealing."

"Hmmm." Fairy Geraldine looked thoughtful. "Perhaps. I was wondering about a magic porridge pot. One needs to be practical these days…"

Fairy Jacqueline gave her a sour look. "After

what happened to the kettle, my dear, I think you should leave kitchen utensils alone."

"What FUN!" Fairy Josephine twirled on her tiptoes. "I do love parties." She paused mid-twirl. "Oh! Do you think they'll remember to invite the Hag? There's bound to be trouble if they don't."

"I'm sure it'll be all right," Fairy Geraldine said. "Scrabster's Hump is miles and miles away. I don't expect the Hag even knows there's a new baby."

But Fairy Geraldine was wrong. The Hag was, at that very moment, studying the poster pinned to a tree on the top of Scrabster's Hump.

"So there's a new baby prince," she muttered, "and we're ordered to rejoice. Huh! We'll see about that. What have that fancy lot ever done for me? Nothing, that's what. Nothing. There'll be a Royal Christening, no doubt, and I expect I'll be forgotten. Always am. I've a good mind to go anyway…" She peered more closely at the paper. "Ha! How very convenient! They've given the date: Midsummer's Morning. Well, well, well. I'll be there, invitation or no invitation – and if there's no invitation, I'll make them very, very sorry!"

And she went to look out her books of magic and a large iron cauldron.

Chapter Five

PRINCESS PEONY'S THIRTEENTH BIRTHDAY finally arrived. The attention of the royal household was firmly fixed on the Royal Christening, but her mother blew her a kiss and gave her a frilly pink dress, which Peony immediately hid in a bottom drawer. Her father gave her a nod and a small purse of silver coins, and her sisters produced a card that had a picture of a cake with fourteen candles.

"It'll do for next year as well," Azabelle told her.

Miss Beef wished her many happy returns, and

suggested that a birthday was an excellent day on which to promise to be a good girl, and always do as she was told.

Peony spent the next five days fretting, but at last Monday came rolling round. By two o'clock she was dressed in her coat and hat and ready ... and so was Miss Beef.

"Excuse me," Peony said politely, "but are you going somewhere?"

Miss Beef glared at her. "Don't be so stupid, child. It's your Educational Outing Day. I'm taking you to the churchyard to look at the tombs of your ancestors. You have an unfortunate tendency to indulge in activities designed exclusively for the lower classes. That book you keep under your pillow! 'Pies, Puddings and Pastries' indeed. The tombs of your ancestors will settle your mind before the christening party tomorrow."

"Oh," said Peony. "Thank you for thinking of – of such an interesting idea, but I'd much rather go on my own."

Miss Beef turned a fearsome shade of puce. "On your own? A princess, walking the streets of Grating alone! Have I taught you nothing in the past ten years?"

Peony considered. "Well," she began, "I suppose I do know my times tables, even though I wobble a bit when it's seven times eight. And I know that Father is King of Grating, and he and Mother are thrilled that they've finally got a baby boy after so many girls. And I know there's going to be a massive christening breakfast—"

"Enough!"

Miss Beef had never found Peony an easy child. She was sadly lacking in any sense of her position as a member of the Royal Family. Her sisters were as rude and demanding as all princesses should be; Miss Beef had no idea where Peony's peculiar behaviour had come from.

"Straighten your back and be quiet," she ordered. "We'll hear no more of this nonsense!"

It took Peony nearly an hour to escape. Miss Beef held the princess's arm in an iron grip all the way to the churchyard, and only let her go when they were finally standing in front of the enormous marble monument to Peony's ancestors. Peony, who was feeling more and more frustrated, was wondering if she would ever get away, when Miss Beef began fishing in her bag for her spectacles.

"Now, where did I put them? I'm sure they're here somewhere … aha! Here they are. Now, let me read you the inscription. Such a splendid list of virtues! 'Nobility, superiority, occasional recognition of the grateful poor'. I suggest you make a note, Peony... Peony?" The governess stared. "Where is she? Where's she gone? Princess Peony! PEONY! Come back this minute!"

But Peony was already out of earshot. She was running, running as fast as she could go. Out of the churchyard, into the high street – narrowly avoiding a carriage pulled by a couple of high-stepping gryphons –

and swerving into a narrow lane. On she ran, looking this way and that for something or somewhere she could recognise. At last she was forced

to admit that she was lost, and
she stopped to ask a passing
gnome if he knew where
the library was.

"The library? First
on the right, second
on the left … that'll be
quickest."

Five minutes later Peony was
outside the library door. Taking a deep breath, she
walked in.

It was nothing like she remembered. The
neatly stacked shelves were now a tumble of
books in tottering heaps and chaotic piles, and
the library desk was covered in dirty cups and
plates. A giant was lying back in the librarian's
chair, fast asleep with his mouth wide open, and a
small pig was rootling in the litter of empty sweet
wrappers spread around the giant's enormous feet.

"Oh dear," Peony said. "Oh dear!"

A small squeak from behind a book stack made her turn, and she found herself looking at Miss Denzil … but a very different Miss Denzil from the neat little person she had met years before. This Miss Denzil was as untidy as the library she worked in, with a dirty apron and wild tangled hair – but her eyes were still kind.

"Can I help you, Miss?" she asked.

Peony fished in the pocket of her coat and brought out *A Thousand Simple Recipes for Pies, Puddings and Pastries*. "I'm so sorry, but I've had this a very long time," she said, "and I know it by heart. I've learnt how to make a perfect cherry pie, and I'm quite good at biscuits. I'd like something different, please. Could you suggest a book about knitting?"

Miss Denzil took a sharp breath. "Oh! Oh oh OH! It's YOU! The little princess! But you've grown so tall!"

"I'm thirteen," Peony said. "I was nine the last time I was here." She shook her head. "We were never allowed to come back … I don't know why. I wanted to, ever so much, but Miss Beef said one visit to a library was more than enough for any respectable princess. She says reading gives people ideas, and no princess needs those." She leant forward. "But I don't agree. Not at all. What do you think?"

The assistant librarian hadn't been asked what she thought about anything since Lionel Longbeard had been taken away, and she was flustered. "Oh! Um … I'm sure you're right, dear." Then, remembering Lionel, she added, "Dear Mr Longbeard always said that books are essential for widening the mind. He knew so much – he must have read most of the books in this library."

"Well, my mind needs a LOT of widening," Peony said. "But who's Mr Longbeard?"

Tears sprang into Miss Denzil's eyes. "The previous librarian, dear. The dwarf who told you there are lots of books about cooking."

"He was kind." Peony nodded. "Very kind. Usually no one said a word when we went on our visits. I used to think nobody in Grating could talk. Is Mr Longbeard here? I'd like to thank him."

Miss Denzil opened and closed her mouth in consternation. How could she tell this girl that Lionel Longbeard was in her father's dungeons, and it was all her doing? "Erm…" she hedged. "Erm…"

"Stoopid dwarf." The giant had woken up and heard Peony's question. "Stoopid dwarf did speaking out of turn to some ol' princessy person." He chuckled. "Out of job, into dungeon … stoopid! That'll teach him."

Peony went very pale and clutched her book to her chest. She looked at Miss Denzil with agonised eyes. "Is that true? He was put in a dungeon just for being kind to me?"

Miss Denzil put an apologetic hand on Peony's arm. "My dear, he spoke to you. He broke the rules…"

"But … but that's the most dreadfully awful thing I've ever heard!" Peony's voice was shaking, and she too had tears in her eyes. "I'm so sorry! Oh, I'm so terribly, TERRIBLY sorry…"

And she rushed out of the library, leaving the cookery book on the counter.

Chapter Six

QUEEN DILYS HAD A HEADACHE. A very bad headache. Preparing a glittering christening breakfast was difficult, particularly as King Thoroughgood insisted on changing the arrangements every five minutes. She was lying in her boudoir, the curtains drawn and a lavender-soaked handkerchief on her forehead, when there was an urgent knocking on the door.

"Your Majesty! Your Majesty!"

The queen gave a faint moan. "I'm not well, Miss Beef. Come back later."

"But Your Majesty, that bad girl Peony has run away!"

Queen Dilys clutched her head. *That's so typical of Peony*, she thought. *The child is nothing but trouble!* Staggering to the door, she opened it to find a flushed and angry Miss Beef standing outside.

"She vanished, Your Majesty," Miss Beef snapped. "I turned my back for a mere second – and she was gone!"

"Where is she now?" Peony's mother was irritated rather than anxious.

Miss Beef was saved from replying by the sound of running feet, and Peony exploded into the room.

"MOTHER! The most awful thing has happened and it's all my fault! You've got to do something or I'll absolutely burst – I know I will!"

The queen collapsed onto her chaise longue. "Peony, what ARE you talking about?"

"It's the librarian, Mother! He's in a dungeon and he shouldn't be! We've got to get him out –

he hasn't done anything wrong, he was trying to help me!"

"A librarian?" Queen Dilys's eyebrows rose. "But why should we worry about a librarian? Really, Peony! I thought it was something serious."

"But it IS serious!" Peony was almost shouting, and her mother sank back, holding her handkerchief to her aching head.

"Peony – that's enough. Quite enough! I don't want to hear another word. Whatever this librarian's done, I'm sure he deserved it, and if he didn't it really isn't any of your business. Now, Miss Beef – kindly do what you're paid to do and take my daughter away." And the queen closed her eyes.

Peony stared at her mother. "How can you say that? How CAN you?

That's just WRONG—"

Miss Beef stepped forward, a steely look in her eyes. "That's enough, Peony!" She seized the princess by the wrist. Peony was taken by surprise; by the time she realised what was happening she was being hauled down the marble corridor to her room. Opening the door, Miss Beef pushed her inside, and a moment later a furious Princess Peony heard a key turn in the lock.

"Wait! Let me out!" she called, but there was no answer. She rushed to the balcony, but she was too high up to jump, and below her was the rose garden, thick with thorns.

"I suppose this must be a little bit how poor Mr Longbeard feels," Peony told herself. "But a dungeon would be much, much worse…"

She sat down on the edge of her bed and looked round. It was a pretty room, with everything a princess might want, but she was now seeing it in a different light. "It only goes to show how much my mind needs widening. I didn't even know there was a dungeon in the palace. That's so dreadful … and Father sent Mr Longbeard there just for speaking to me!" Peony began to feel an uncomfortable sensation in her stomach. "Oh dear," she said. "Oh dear. Does that mean I'm the daughter of a tyrant? Or … or could Father just have made a mistake? But I don't think he makes mistakes." She sat up straighter. "I have to talk to him. It's much better to sort these things out. I can tell him it was my fault, and then he'll have to set Mr Longbeard free."

A sound from outside made the princess run to the balcony. A heavily laden cart was rolling up the drive, coming to a halt outside the kitchen door. The burly driver and his mate climbed down and began carrying boxes and bundles into the palace.

"Oh! I'd almost forgotten. Tomorrow's the christening party!" At once Peony's mood lifted. It would be the ideal moment to ask a favour.

Another cart pulled up behind the first, and Peony watched with interest as a particularly large box was unloaded. One of the gnomes took off the lid, revealing a splendid christening cake, covered in icing twirls and curls and fancy icing lace.

The gnome wiped his brow. "Phew! Weighs a ton!"

His companion grunted. "Let's get it inside."

A moment later the two of them were staggering into the palace with their precious load, leaving a dwarf in charge of the cart. An idea flashed into Peony's head, and she leant dangerously far over the balcony.

"Excuse me!" she called. "Excuse me, Mr Dwarf – can I ask you something?"

The dwarf looked round to see where the voice was coming from. When he saw Peony he went bright red and crouched down in his seat, making it very obvious that he was trying to look invisible. When his companions came back he said something to them in a low voice, and all four of them turned and stared up at Peony. She gave a cheerful wave, but their expressions remained stony. The Royal Family, demanding, unfriendly and convinced of their own importance, were not popular.

Peony, knowing nothing of this, was baffled. She tried waving again, but the four were busy unloading the rest of their goods as fast as they could, and a moment later the two carts were rattling down the drive.

They looked at me as if they hated me, Peony thought. *But why? Do they know about Mr Longbeard? Oh, I absolutely HAVE to do something. I've got to get out of here – I need to talk to Father right now this minute!*

Chapter Seven

WHILE PEONY WAS WORRYING about Lionel
Longbeard, the Hag was brooding. No invitation
had arrived, and she was growing angrier by the
day … a state she much enjoyed, as it gave her a
reason to practise her darkest and most unpleasant
spells. She had half-filled her cauldron with a
distillation of deadly nightshade and essence of
poisonous toadstool and, as each day passed
and no invitation came rattling through her
letterbox, she added something more disgusting
to the contents.

   "Wooooo…" she sang happily as she stirred the

new ingredients in. **"Woooo … woooo … woooo!**
Let the brew get ever stronger … let them
suffer ever longer…"

The Hag did, however, have a practical
problem: her snakeskin dress didn't fit. She had
been eating unusually well; a few weeks earlier a
goatherd had driven his unfortunate flock into the
caves beneath Scrabster's Hump in order to save
them from a terrible thunderstorm. What he was
not saving them from was a hungry Hag: not a
single goat made its way back to the grassy slopes.
The goatherd, unwilling to search the caves,
packed up his goatherd's whistle and went off to
be a plumber. The Hag had eaten three enormous
meals a day and doubled in size as she read her
books of dark magic. Now, as she tried the dress
on, even the spiders sniggered.

"I'll have to let it out," she said. "What a bore!"

Not being much of a seamstress, the Hag
decided to use magic. The results would not be

as reliable as a good stout running stitch, but the christening party was the following day and she had no choice.

"Wooooo wooooo!" she chanted. **"Wooooo wooooo!"**

The dress obligingly grew … and grew. The Hag tutted crossly and tried again. This time the dress developed a surprising number of pockets, together with a Victorian bustle.

"Wooooo!" the Hag ordered. **"WOOOOO!"**

The bustle fell off, but the pockets remained. No amount of wand waving could remove them and at last the Hag, by now in a terrible temper, gave up.

"Stupid thing! I'll have to wear it as it is," she muttered. "It's all that king's fault. And that queen. If they'd sent me an invitation to their ridiculous christening party I'd have thought about ordering a new dress … but I'll make them pay! Oh, how I'll make them pay! I'll steal their precious little baby, that's what I'll do – and I'll not give the boy back until they're weeping and wailing and begging on their knees." An evil smile crept slowly over her face. "And I know just how I'm going to do it…"

She opened a drawer in the kitchen dresser. A small warty toad scrambled out and made a hopeful leap for freedom, but the Hag caught it and popped it in an empty milk jug. Digging deeper in the drawer she pulled out several balls of musty-smelling green string, and her smile grew even nastier. "Sleeping twine," she muttered. "I'll make bunches and bunches of sleeping twine … and the potion should be just about ready. **Dip it in, dip it deep – that'll send the fools to sleep!**"

The Fairy Godmothers of Murk were also worrying about their dresses. "Everyone in red, do you think?" Fairy Geraldine suggested.

"Blue might be more suitable for a boy," Fairy Josephine said. "Or is that too obvious?"

Fairy Jacqueline was looking in the wardrobe. "Ridiculously obvious. What about a nice bright orange? Very ladylike and most becoming."

The other two fairies went to look. "That is pretty," Fairy Geraldine agreed. "But I do love red."

"Blue," Fairy Josephine said. "Definitely blue!"

Fairy Jacqueline pulled out a bright orange dress with a flourish. "Well, I want to wear this. You two can do as you want." And

slamming the wardrobe door shut, she stalked off with her dress over her arm.

Fairy Geraldine shook her head. "Temper, temper!"

Fairy Josephine sighed. "If only the king or the queen would ask us to grant a couple of wishes. That would cheer her up no end, even if they were only little ones."

"Maybe they will at the christening party." Fairy Geraldine was always optimistic. "After all, they did invite us."

Fairy Josephine looked doubtful. "Perhaps. Let's hope for the best. So you're going to wear red?"

"Of course." Fairy Geraldine twirled a curl. "And I suppose you're wearing blue?"

"Naturally," Fairy Josephine said. "And I think we'll look lovely. Just like a bunch of summer flowers!"

Chapter Eight

THERE WAS TROUBLE in the palace as well. One
of the boxes delivered that afternoon was full
of dresses and shoes, and the six sisters were
fighting over them.

"I'm the oldest, so I get first choice!" Azabelle
declared.

"But that's not fair! You ALWAYS get first
choice!" Bettina's face was very red. "We should
take turns!"

"All right," Azabelle agreed. "I'll have the first
turn at choosing!"

There was a protesting wail from her sisters,

and Emmadine snatched up a dress from the pile
on the floor. "I want THIS one!" she said.

"But that's the one *I* want!" Fabrizia seized the
dress and tugged. Emmadine refused to let go,
and a moment later there was a ripping noise.

"Now look what you've done!" Fabrizia glared
at her sister. "You've ruined it! Now there won't be
enough to go round!"

"Yes there will." Clothilde counted out the

remaining dresses. "One two three, four five six! They must have sent an extra one."

Donnetta looked doubtful. "What about the freak?"

"Peony?" Azabelle shrugged. "Mother gave her a dress for her birthday. She can wear that."

"But these are all blue and white," Donnetta objected. "Peony's birthday dress is pink."

"Whose side are you on?" Clothilde frowned

at her sister. "If you're so worried about Peony, give her your dress! And then YOU can explain why you don't look like the rest of us!"

"The freak doesn't need to know," Bettina said. "We'll just tell her Mother's expecting her to wear pink."

This seemed to Donnetta to be a happy solution, and she joined in the scrum to choose the prettiest dress. Further inspection revealed that the dresses were all very pretty, and the bickering died away.

"Who's going to tell Peony?" Clothilde asked once peace was restored.

"Fabrizia ought to tell her," Emmadine said. "She tore the dress."

"No I didn't." Fabrizia was outraged. "You did!"

Emmadine shrugged. "We'll both go."

The two princesses were surprised to find Peony's door was locked.

"Peony! Open the door!" Fabrizia ordered.

"I can't." Peony had her eye to the keyhole. "Miss Beef locked me in and she took the key away with her."

"So you won't be coming to the christening tomorrow?" Emmadine could see an answer to their problem.

"Yes I will!" Peony was indignant. "She's got to let me out before then."

"Oh." Emmadine, disappointed, sagged against the door. Fabrizia pushed her out of the way.

"Peony? Listen! You're to wear your birthday dress tomorrow – the pink one Mother gave you."

There was a moment's silence, and then Peony said, "I thought Father wanted us all dressed the same. Blue and white dresses … I'm sure that's what he said."

"He must have changed his mind," Fabrizia began, but Emmadine seized her arm.

"You don't need to explain," she said. "Come

on!" And she and her sister sped away.

Peony was left staring at the keyhole. "Bother," she said. "I hate that dress. It makes me look like a boiled prawn." She opened her chest of drawers and pulled the dress out. It looked even worse than before, as it was now creased and wrinkled. "Oh dear. I'll have to try to borrow an iron. I do wish it wasn't so terribly frilly!" She tweaked at a frill and it came away under her fingers. She gave another tentative pull and yet more of the frill unravelled. "It's not very well made," she said disapprovingly, and she looked more closely. "It's just tacked on! It's yards and yards of ribbon held on with a single thread! I wonder... Oh, I do wonder. Let's see if I'm right!"

Peony gave a hearty tug and was rewarded with handfuls of frilled silk. It took her five minutes to remove enough for her plan. Plaiting three lengths together made a substantial rope; the princess tied it to a bedpost, then heaved on it. "It looks strong enough," she told herself. "And there's only one way to find out if it is..."

She went to the window. Another couple of carts were being unloaded outside the kitchen door, and Peony was forced to wait until they were empty. As they rattled away she pulled the ribbon rope across the room and tossed it over the balcony. She was pleased to see it almost reached the ground. *At least I won't have to jump the last bit*, she thought. *I do wish it wasn't roses down there, though. They look horribly prickly!*

After one last tug to test the rope's strength, Princess Peony began to climb down.

On the other side of the courtyard, Basil was watching. "Interesting," he said thoughtfully. "Very interesting…"

Chapter Nine

KING THOROUGHGOOD was in a bad mood. The christening breakfast was to take place in the royal banqueting hall, and he had spent the day storming up and down it, shouting at the various trolls, maids, dwarves, pageboys and gnomes who were putting up tables, arranging flowers, polishing plates and sorting knives, forks and spoons. The magnificent cake was in position; the prime minister, who was scuttling behind the king trying to keep up with his master's instructions, attempted to lighten the atmosphere.

"The cake's very fine, Your Majesty. Very

fine indeed. A most excellent choice!"

The king's brow darkened. "It's too small. It should be bigger! Much bigger."

"Yes! Yes of course, Your Majesty. Should I order another one?" The prime minister bowed very low, keeping his fingers crossed. At this late stage another cake would be impossible. Fortunately a gnome carrying a large vase of multicoloured flowers scurried past, and the cake was immediately forgotten.

"Blue and white!" the king roared. "Blue and white! Does nobody ever listen to me? I said no reds or yellows or pinks or purples! The decoration is to be blue and white, and ONLY blue and white!" He snatched at a pink rose, threw it on the floor and stamped on it. The gnome was so surprised that he dropped the vase, and it was at this unfortunate moment that Princess Peony came flying through the door.

"Father!" she called. "Father! I have to talk to

you – it's really, really, REALLY important!"

It took King Thoroughgood a long moment to recognise his tangle-haired and breathless daughter. An argument with the thorniest of the roses had left her arms scratched and her dress torn. "Peony! How dare you come rushing in looking like ... like a PEASANT!"

"Oh, never mind what I look like!" Peony seized her father's arm. "Father, you've made a terrible mistake and it's all my fault!"

"A mistake?" The king's frown grew darker. He was not a man who made mistakes.

"The librarian! It was ages and ages ago, but I've only just found out about it. You had him thrown into a dungeon and he was only trying to help! Please, Father – PLEASE let him out!"

Even a king has difficult days, and this had been an especially difficult day for King Thoroughgood. Everything had gone wrong that could possibly go wrong – and now Princess

Peony was demanding something that was not just ridiculous, but positively treasonable.

"Absolutely not!" the king thundered. "Absolutely NOT!" He swung round to the prime minister. "Skeldith! Lock my daughter in her room!"

"If you try, Mr Skeldith, I'll … I'll BITE YOU!" Peony's glare was even more threatening than her father's, and Skeldith backed hastily away. "Father, you've got to listen to me!"

Her father was purple with rage. He was the king. He was His Royal Highness King Thoroughgood – and he was being defied in public by a girl in a torn and dirty dress. He knew the servants were winking at each other, sniggering, laughing at him… It was too much.

"Guards!" Two substantial trolls came running.

"Guards, take the princess away and put her in the dungeon – the dungeon for Those Who Speak Out Of Turn." The king scowled at his daughter.

"Perhaps THAT will teach you to mind your manners!"

As the guards carried Peony away, she called, "I'll be looking for Mr Longbeard, Father! It wasn't his fault! I'll tell him you'll let him out very soon!"

Queen Dilys, woken from her nap by an agitated Miss Beef, had hardly heard the news of Peony's escape before King Thoroughgood appeared in the doorway. "That girl is out of control," he raged. "Do you hear, Dilys? Out of control!" Seeing Miss Beef, he turned a darker shade of purple. "And what do you have to say for yourself, woman? My daughter is running riot, and you're nowhere to be seen!"

"I don't think you need worry, dear," the queen said in her most soothing tone. She can't have gone far—"

"She went TOO far! She came running into the banqueting hall and accused me – ME! – of making a mistake! In front of all the servants! I won't have it, I tell you!" The king was pacing up and down. "She needs to be taught a lesson!"

Miss Beef, eager to account for herself, nodded enthusiastically. "That's why I locked her in her room, Your Majesty—"

"And much good that did," the king snapped. For a brief moment it occurred to him that Peony had shown remarkable ingenuity in escaping, but he crushed the thought. "Useless! Totally useless. But I've dealt with it. A strong hand, that's what's needed… I've had her thrown in the dungeons."

"The dungeons?" Queen Dilys looked startled. "My dear – she's our daughter! A princess!"

"Then she must learn to behave like one. And if those who are paid to control her can't do it, then I will!" King Thoroughgood gave Miss Beef a final glare and strode away.

"This is all most unfortunate." The queen fanned herself with her handkerchief. "It's the christening tomorrow morning! Will he allow Peony out in time, do you think? Goodness! What will people say if she's not there?"

Miss Beef was seething with righteous anger. "I don't wish to criticise, Your Majesty, but I've never, in all my years as a governess, met such a wild, self-willed girl. I've done my best, Your Majesty – but I do not expect to be blamed for such totally impossible behaviour!"

Queen Dilys looked vague. "I'm sure you're right, Miss Beef. Now, if you could just go and see that the girls' dresses have arrived safely? I absolutely MUST close my eyes, or I'll be a complete wreck tomorrow…" And she waved the fuming Miss Beef out of the room before sinking back on her bed.

Chapter Ten

PEONY WAS INSPECTING her new surroundings with
interest. The guards were marching her down
a long, dark corridor; on either side were heavy
iron doors, each with a small grille. Occasional
mutterings could be heard from inside, including
a request for "Hot buttered toast, and be quick
about it!"

Peony was relieved to see that most of the
doors were open and the cells empty. *Maybe
Father doesn't use the dungeons very often,* she
thought. *And maybe the prisoners have done
unspeakably dreadful things.* She turned to one of

the guards. "What did he do?" she asked, pointing at a door with a remarkable number of padlocks.

The guard shrugged. "Ask the king. He put 'im there. Been there months."

"Stole a cheese," the other guard volunteered. "Trouble was, it was due to go to the palace. Upset His Majesty something shocking."

"Oh." Peony found it hard to believe that the theft of a cheese deserved such harsh punishment, and her face was thoughtful as she continued down the corridor.

The dungeon for Those Who Speak Out Of Turn was the very last door. The hairier guard produced a large key and turned it in the lock with much huffing and puffing. "'Ere!" he announced as the door finally swung open. "Enjoy!" He pushed Peony inside and slammed the door behind her. A moment later the grille slid open. "Supper'll be in a while, Miss. Buttered beans. Ain't no toast." And the grille was shut.

"Buttered beans?" Peony said wonderingly. "I don't think I've ever eaten buttered beans. This is definitely widening my mind. Brrrrr! It's very cold in here."

She looked round and saw the stone walls were glistening with damp. Some attempt at comfort had been made: six iron beds heaped with rough

blankets were ranged around a feeble fire at one end of the room, and there were clean rushes on the floor. Light filtered down from narrow windows high under the rafters; Peony immediately squinted up to see if she could squeeze through. Deciding she couldn't climb the smooth grey walls, she made her way towards the fire.

Coming closer, she discovered that two of the beds were occupied. A faint snoring came from both, but the occupants were buried so deep under the blankets it was impossible to make out who they might be. Rubbing her hands together, Peony turned to the fire.

"Is there any more coal?" she asked loudly. "This fire is useless … I'm freezing, and I'm sure you are too."

There was no answer, but the snoring stopped.

"I'm Peony, by the way," she went on. "I'm looking for a Mr Lionel Longbeard. I owe him an apology."

The blankets on the nearer bed heaved and a deep voice said, "An apology? Nobody ever apologises round here. And who would want to apologise to a librarian? Who ARE you?"

The blankets parted and a head emerged. The nose was so remarkable that Peony had to force herself not to stare. *Now my mind is really widening,* she thought. *I've met trolls, and dwarves, and gnomes – but I've never ever seen a nose like this.* She stepped forward and dropped a little curtsy. "How do you do? I'm Peony. Might I ask who you are?"

"Horrington," said the head. "Horrington Wells. Stand still, child. I need to look at you. And you'll want to look at me. Everyone does. It's only to be expected. Horrington Wells is a rarity, an exception … a vision. We will stare at each other for – shall we say, forty seconds?"

Peony felt compelled to curtsy a second time. "Certainly…"

"Then let us begin."

Horrington's face was very long, not unlike a gloomy horse. His nose was not only large, but a bright strawberry red, and the straggles of hair were rust-coloured. His gaze was fixed on Peony's face, and he did not blink until he gave a sigh and said, "Child! Our forty seconds is complete. Tell me, what have you learnt?"

"Erm…" Peony considered. "I think you are … very different—" She stopped, wondering if she had been rude, but Horrington seemed pleased rather than offended. He pushed the blankets aside and swung himself upright, and Peony saw that he was extraordinarily tall and very thin. He was dressed in red and yellow velvet, so faded and old that Peony wondered how it held together.

"I am indeed different, child," Horrington said. "I am, as you may see by my attire, a jester. I tell jokes. Let me prove it to you. Answer me this: what fish only comes out at night?"

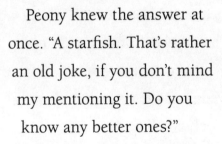

Peony knew the answer at once. "A starfish. That's rather an old joke, if you don't mind my mentioning it. Do you know any better ones?"

"I fear not." Horrington shook his head. "And I see you are one who speaks her mind. Is that why you have joined us?"

"Oh yes," Peony said with feeling. "Father got cross with me and ordered the guards to bring me here – but I don't mind because I want to tell Mr Longbeard how sorry I am." She looked across at the other bed and lowered her voice. "Is that him?"

By way of an answer Horrington leant across and tweaked at the bedcovers. "My friend – are you awake?"

"My knees hurt." The voice was decidedly grumpy. "Rheumatism. That's what it is … rheumatism. From the damp."

Peony's eyes widened. "Mr Longbeard! It's Peony! Don't you remember me? I met you in your lovely library…"

There was an eruption of bed covers, blankets and feathers, and up sat a tousled dwarf dressed in blue pyjamas. He stared at the princess. "WHAT? I've never seen you before in my life!"

"But you have!" Peony leant over the end of the

bed. "I came with my sisters and Miss Beef, and I asked you a question – I didn't know it wasn't allowed! And I'm so very sorry, because you were punished for being kind and helpful and that should never ever have happened…" She paused as the dwarf scrabbled under his thin pillow. Pulling out a pair of wire spectacles, he balanced them on the end of his nose.

"Let me see … let me see… Yes… Perhaps I do remember. You're Princess Peony."

He took his spectacles off, cleaned them on his pyjamas, and put them back on again. "And you've come to say you're sorry… Well, well, well."

Peony clasped her hands together. "I tried to tell Father he made a terrible mistake putting you in a dungeon, Mr Longbeard, but he wouldn't listen."

She saw the dwarf's shoulders droop and ran to his side. "Mr Longbeard, I'll do everything I can to get you out – I promise."

Chapter Eleven

As Peony did her best to soothe Lionel Longbeard, Horrington Wells raised an eyebrow. "Do I understand that you're one of the princesses, child?"

"I'm the youngest," Peony told him. "Well – baby Vicenzo's the youngest now, of course."

"A boy?" Horrington was surprised.

"He's the sweetest baby!" Peony's face lit up. "I just wish I could play with him—"

She was interrupted by the sound of clanking and rattling, and a moment later the dungeon door swung open and the prime minister edged inside. He looked round nervously, and cleared his throat.

"Princess Peony," he began, but got no further. Peony had jumped to her feet when she heard the door being unlocked, and now she ran to him and clutched at his arm.

"Skeldith! Dear Mr Skeldith! Have you come to let Mr Longbeard out?"

Skeldith cleared his throat a second time. He was of the decided opinion that visiting a dungeon was not something a man in his position should be asked to do. The king, however, had been insistent.

"I regret to say, Princess, that is not the message His Majesty wished me to convey. His Majesty wished me to ask if you were sorry for your – *ahem!* – behaviour. If that is the case you may return to the palace. Ahem. And His Majesty would, I was instructed to say, expect a personal apology in the morning."

"An apology?" Peony stared at him. "Whatever for? All I did was ask him to set Mr Longbeard free!"

Skeldith coughed. "*Ahem*. I can only repeat His Majesty's message, Princess."

Peony took a deep breath, marched to an empty bed and sat down. "Tell my father I'm staying here. I'm not leaving until Mr Longbeard leaves with me." And she folded her arms.

The prime minister was horrified. "But Princess—" he began.

"No." Peony shook her head. "I've made up my mind." Seeing Skeldith's expression, she fished in her pockets for a pencil. "I'll write a message, and then you won't have to tell Father yourself. Has anyone got a piece of paper?"

Horrington produced an old envelope from the depths of his battered tunic. "Here, child."

"Thank you." Peony took the envelope and began to write while Skeldith stood waiting, shifting uneasily from foot to foot.

Lionel Longbeard pushed aside the blankets, looking anxious. "Princess! There's no need for you to stay here—"

"There is," Peony said. "I've got to make Father listen." She finished her last sentence with a decisive full stop and held the envelope out to Skeldith. "Tell him this is from me." She gave the prime minister a doubtful look. "You will give it to him, won't you?"

Skeldith took the envelope with relief. With luck he could hand it to the king then remove himself with sufficient speed to avoid the inevitable explosion. "Of course, Princess." He turned and scurried out.

Peony shook her head sadly. "Poor Skeldith. He's scared of Father." She sighed. "It's because Father gets into such terrible rages … and when he's in a rage he threatens all kinds of things. He doesn't really mean them, though." She saw Lionel Longbeard's face and paused. "But he does, doesn't he? Oh dear." She turned to Horrington. "Tell me truthfully – do you think my father's a tyrant? I'm beginning to have a horrible feeling that he might be."

Horrington took his time considering his answer. "Most kings like to have their own way, child."

Peony was very still.

"I see," she said, and took a deep breath. "Yes. I see. I expect you thought it would be rude to say yes … but I understand."

Horrington looked at Peony with concern. "Princess, are you all right?"

"Yes…" Peony sniffed and wiped her nose with the back of her hand. "Yes," she said more firmly. "And I did say I wanted to widen my mind." She sniffed again. "The lady in the library told me how books can do that, Mr Longbeard."

"Miss Denzil?" The librarian brightened. "Have you seen her? Is she well?"

Peony managed a watery smile. "Yes … I saw her this afternoon! That's why I'm here. I didn't know what had happened to you. I ran to tell Father—"

"And he didn't listen," Lionel said, and the light in his eyes died. "I'm afraid you're wasting your time, Princess."

Peony stood up straight. "I'm not. And I'm

not scared of Father.
I won't leave until he
sets us all free." She
glanced at Horrington.
"I'm sorry, I never
asked you why you're
here. Have you been
here long?"

Horrington gave a
wry smile. "Long enough. I foolishly believed that
your father might wish to employ a jester."

"A jester?" Peony shook her head. "Oh dear.
Father hates jokes."

"So I discovered. He said he would only give
me the position of court jester if I could make
him laugh, and I failed. Dismally. My last joke
offended him so much he sent me here."

Peony looked at him with interest. "What was
the joke?"

"Why is a king like a child at school?"

"Ummm…" Peony thought of Miss Beef and her endless list of dos and don'ts. "Because … because… I can't guess. Something to do with being a good ruler?"

Horrington chuckled. "That would have been a better answer, perhaps. No, I told him that a king and a child at school both need to study their subjects well if they wish to grow old and wise."

Peony blinked. "Ah… No. He wouldn't care for that at all. What was it you said – that kings like to have their own way? Father thinks he's always right." She stared into the flickering flames of the fire. "It would do Father good to be a little wiser, wouldn't it?"

"We could all do with being a little wiser," the jester said, and Lionel Longbeard snorted.

"Some more than others," he said sourly.

Chapter Twelve

PREPARATIONS FOR THE CHRISTENING breakfast
went on … and on. King Thoroughgood grew
increasingly irritable. Nothing was big enough,
fine enough or blue and white enough. By late
that evening everyone was exhausted, and Queen
Dilys was despairing.

"It'll be a disaster," she wailed. "A complete
disaster!"

The king scowled at her. "It will not! I won't
allow it. My son will be christened in a cloud of
glory!"

Queen Dilys shook her head and retired to

her bedroom with a hot-water bottle. The king continued to issue orders as the night crept on, and the first light of dawn could be seen over the horizon when he finally announced that all was ready. The servants dragged themselves away while he made one last tour of the royal banqueting hall, the wilting prime minister at his side.

"Excellent!" King Thoroughgood nodded. "Excellent! I think raising my throne up higher and surrounding it with flowers was an inspired idea. I'm glad I thought of it. The queen and the princesses will sit below me, of course—" He stopped, and the prime minister held his breath. "SEVEN chairs?" The king counted again, and his expression of extreme self-satisfaction faded. "SEVEN? But I have a queen, and I have seven daughters. Skeldith! Where is the eighth chair?"

Skeldith wriggled like a worm on the end of a pin. "Erm … I told them to take Princess

Peony's chair away, Your Majesty…"

King Thoroughgood stared at him. "What do you mean?" A thought came to him, and he slowly turned a deeper and deeper shade of purple. "Are you telling me that my daughter is still in the dungeon?"

The unfortunate prime minister nodded.

"Did you not pass on my instruction that she was to apologise?"

Skeldith's teeth began to chatter. "Yes, Your Majesty…" He fished in his pocket and brought out the crumpled envelope. "She … she asked me to give you this. Um … if Your Majesty has no further need of me, I'll be off—"

"WAIT!" The king snatched the paper and read it. Then he read it again, and then a third time. Finally he tore the envelope into little tiny pieces, threw them on the floor and stamped on them. "I will not be dictated to by my daughter!" he roared. "I will NOT! If she wishes to befriend the rogues and criminals that fill my dungeons, then let her. She is not to be released until she is willing to make a full apology, and that, Skeldith, is that! Do I make myself clear?"

The prime minister nodded.

"Now sweep up this mess! And make sure you're here to greet our visitors when they arrive." The king strode away, leaving Skeldith to find a dustpan and brush.

In the dungeon for Those Who Speak Out Of Turn, the previous evening's activities had been more cheerful. Peony had heaped the fire with coal and it was burning brightly. When Lionel Longbeard complained that she had used an entire week's coal ration she smiled happily at him. "But Mr Longbeard, I've decided: I think we ought to escape, all of us together. And I think it ought to be tonight, so we might as well make ourselves comfortable. When do we get our buttered beans, by the way? I'm starving! And what do we get for breakfast? If we're still here, that is, which I hope we won't be."

"Buttered beans," Horrington told her. "It's buttered beans for breakfast, dinner and supper.

A little unimaginative, I always think." He gave Peony a hopeful glance. "Ahem. Which vegetable is the oldest of all vegetables?"

Lionel groaned. "Beans, because they've always been there. You've told me that one every day since you got here."

"Buttered beans ALL the time?" Peony stared at Horrington. "Goodness! We certainly do need to escape. As soon as we're all free I'll make you the very best cherry pie ever." She looked up. "Now, we should make a plan. We could all squeeze through those windows, so we have to decide on a way of getting up there." She paused. "I've already escaped once today, you know. If this goes on, I'll soon be an expert!"

Lionel Longbeard sighed. "Don't you think we've already considered escaping, Princess?"

"Oh! I'm so sorry! Of course you have." Peony

flushed. "I didn't mean to be bossy."

Horrington frowned at the dwarf. "An extra point of view is always welcome. What did you have in mind?"

"Well…" Peony stepped back and stared up at the windows. Then she turned and looked at the iron beds. "I'm thinking," she said slowly, "that if we upend one of the beds it would reach quite high. And you, Mr Wells, are very, very tall. And if I were to climb on your shoulders – if you don't object, that is – I might be able to get to the window. And look! You see each window has a central bar? If I tie a rope around that, you and Mr Longbeard can climb up after me!"

"Very clever." The dwarf sounded less than enthusiastic. "There's just one problem: we don't have a rope."

Peony clapped her hands. "Oh, but we do! We can tear up the sheets off the beds, and tie them into a rope!"

There was a thoughtful silence.

"Do you know," Horrington said at last, "I think it might work…"

Lionel Longbeard nodded. "I apologise, Princess Peony. I spoke too hastily."

"Then let's begin," Peony said – but at that moment there was a rattling at the door.

"Buttered beans!" said a gruff voice, and a large troll came stomping in with a tray. "'Ere you is. Extra portions, seeing as you've got a royal for company. Enjoy!"

The buttered beans were not as delicious as Peony had imagined. They came from a pot that the guards used to wash their socks, and had a curious woolly texture. All the same, she ate them with a smile. "Do they come and collect the dishes tonight?" she asked.

Lionel Longbeard nodded. "They'll be back in a couple of hours."

"Then we'll wait," Peony said, "and escape as soon as they've gone."

"A nap might be wise," Horrington suggested. "Sometimes they don't come until quite late."

Peony yawned. "That's a good idea. It's been a busy day." She chose a bed and snuggled herself down under the blankets. "You will wake me, won't you? As soon as the guards have been?"

"No need to worry," Horrington assured her. "Those trolls have feet of lead. And they enjoy slamming the door."

"That's all right then," Peony said, and as soon as her head hit the pillow she was asleep.

Horrington sat down on his own bed. "A dear child. It's lucky, my friend, that she's so different from her father."

The dwarf nodded. "But is she right? Will she be able to escape?"

"It's possible." The tall man measured the wall with his eye. "But if I understand you correctly, friend Lionel, you don't intend to follow the princess to freedom."

"What would I gain?" The dwarf pulled at his beard. "If I leave here without the king's pardon, I can't return to my library. Guards would be sent to find me – I'd be hunted high and low." He gave his companion a sideways look. "As would you."

"And for that reason, I too will be staying here." Horrington looked up at the windows. "But the princess may still win her father round."

"I thought I'd given up hope," Lionel said, "but you're right. That child has determination."

Horrington laughed. "Perhaps she is a little like her father, after all."

Chapter Thirteen

THE DISHES WERE NOT COLLECTED that night. The guards had been presented with one of the barrels of ginger beer and had decided to begin celebrating the christening early. Finding the contents of the barrel not to their taste they had added something a little stronger, and their celebrations lasted long past midnight.

They were exceedingly bleary-eyed when they came stomping down the dungeon corridor early the following morning, wincing at every rattle of their keys. They heaped the dishes from the various cells onto a sticky tray and handed out dry bread and cold beans for breakfast, finally arriving at the dungeon for Those Who Speak Out Of Turn. It took them a while to find the keyhole, and when at last they managed it there was an argument as to which of them would pick up the dishes and which would stand by the door. The sound of their voices woke Peony, and she was sitting up in bed when the larger guard came lumbering in.

"Hello," she said – and then, seeing daylight creeping through the narrow windows, "Oh no! What time is it?"

The guard gawped at her. "Uh?"

Peony jumped out of bed. "What time is it?"

The guard scratched his head. "It's morning."

"But is it early morning?" Peony insisted.

This was too much. The guard's head hurt, and all he wanted to do was sleep for at least two days. "Morning's morning." And he picked up the dirty dishes, dumped down a small bowl of bread and beans and lumbered away.

As the door clanged shut behind him Horrington opened his eyes. "Now's your moment, Princess," he said. "They won't be back for hours. And yes … I believe it's still quite early."

Peony's eyes shone as she pulled the sheet off her bed and began tearing it into strips. "Time to escape! Although," she added wistfully, "it really should have been in the middle of the night if it was going to be a proper escape…"

Half an hour later Peony was balanced precariously on Horrington Wells' shoulders, stretching up to a dungeon window. The rope of torn sheets was tied round her waist, and standing below her was Lionel Longbeard, holding the upended iron bed steady.

"I'm not sure this window opens," she reported. "I might have to break the glass. Do you think there's anyone outside who will hear?"

"Who knows?" Horrington said. "Can you see anything?"

"The window's very dirty," Peony told him, "but I'm almost sure we're at the back of the palace." She rubbed at the glass with her fingers. "Yes! It's the orchard. And I can see the big oak tree. I've always wanted to climb it, but Miss Beef would never let me ... OH! Oh my goodness! How lucky is that? Mr Wells – Mr Longbeard – the window's at ground level! We won't have to climb down the rope once we're outside. It's just a little jump!"

"A little jump is good," Horrington said cautiously. "Do be careful, Princess. Glass is sharp!"

Peony didn't answer. She was tugging at the window catch, trying to force it open. Years of wind and rain had rusted the frame, and as she gave a final heave the entire window fell into the dungeon with a crash, scattering shards of glass over the cold stone floor.

"That'll leave us with a nasty chilly draught on a winter's night," Lionel muttered, but he made sure he spoke too low for Peony to hear. She was already climbing through the gap, pulling the rope behind her. Seconds later she was balanced on the other side, peering back at her two companions.

"It's really easy," she encouraged. "Mr Wells – are you coming next?"

Horrington coughed. "Princess Peony," he said, "you must go alone."

"WHAT?"

It was difficult to see Peony's face, but her tone was one of hurt astonishment. Horrington, still balanced on the end of the iron bedstead, steadied himself against the wall and tried to explain. "Think, dear child. If Lionel and I escape, where will we go? What will your father do when he finds his dungeon empty? Why – send the guards out to catch us, and neither of us has a mind to play cat and mouse for the rest of our lives."

There was the sound of a suppressed sniff, and then Peony said, "But why didn't you tell me before? Why did you let me think we were all going to escape together?"

Horrington sighed. "If we'd told you earlier, would you have agreed to go on your own?"

Peony thought about this. "No," she said slowly. "You're right. I'd have insisted on staying with you … and I still can!" She began to climb back.

"NO!" Horrington shouted, and Peony froze. "Excuse me, Princess, but this is important. You must persuade your father to let us go free. My friend badly needs to return to his library."

Peony looked down at the dwarf. He was still holding on to the bed but he was staring at the floor, shoulders bowed. Even in the half light she could see how old he had become, and how defeated. "Oh, poor Mr Longbeard! Of course I will … I absolutely promise." She paused. "Maybe I ought to be a bit more tactful next time I speak to Father. What do you think?"

Horrington smiled up at her. "Now you come to mention it, you might be right, Princess."

The princess giggled and climbed back out, pulling the rope after her. "They mustn't find out

I've gone. Heap up the blankets on my bed and tell them I'm asleep."

Horrington did his best to bow. "Princess, your ingenuity amazes me."

"I'll come back later and tell you how I'm getting on," Peony promised. "Goodbye for now, Mr Wells. Mr Longbeard – please, PLEASE don't despair!" And then she was gone, taking the sheet rope with her.

The jester jumped down, and together he and the dwarf restored the dungeon to something like its previous appearance. Pillows were stuffed down Peony's bed and the result was convincing enough to fool the guards. The glass they left.

"I shall complain about the dangers of ancient windows," Lionel said, and he nodded at Horrington. "I shall be suitably outraged!"

"Indeed." Horrington yawned. "It's still early, my friend. Go back to sleep. Dream of freedom, and your library…"

Lionel Longbeard looked up at the empty window space. "I think perhaps I will," he said, and he climbed back into his bed with something almost like a smile.

Chapter Fourteen

ONCE OUTSIDE, PEONY WOUND UP the rope and slung it over her shoulder. "I'd better keep this – I might need it," she decided. "And now I'll climb the oak tree. It's too early to go and find Father; he's always grumpy before breakfast. And I can peek in the palace windows from up in the branches, so I'll know when everyone's awake."

She ran through the orchard, jumping to pick any cherries that were low enough to reach, and a moment later she was swinging herself up through the green leaves of the oak tree. The sun had risen over the distant hills and Peony, whistling happily, climbed higher and higher in the summer morning air. A pigeon, disturbed on its branch, fluttered away, and she waved at it. "I always knew this would be a fabulous tree to climb," she said. "Now … how much higher can I go?"

After five minutes' energetic climbing the princess found that she could see not only the palace roof sparkling in the sunshine, but the courtyard and driveway beyond, too.

"Oh my goodness!" Peony gazed round in wonder. As she looked, her eyes caught sight of a distant movement. "Oh," she said. "Isn't that the milk cart?" And she watched it make its way towards the palace. The milk cart was soon followed by three bakers' wagons, and Peony leant back against the tree trunk.

All these things coming to the palace, she thought. *They must be for the christening. What shall I do? Should I see if I can creep back to my bedroom? But what would Father say?* She frowned as she considered. *I've got to find the right moment to talk to him … and not make him angry again. That won't help Mr Longbeard. Maybe I should wait until the christening is over and ask him then. Oh dear. I wish I knew the best thing to do.*

Yet another vehicle appeared, and Peony watched curiously as it slowly trundled up the driveway. *That doesn't look like a delivery cart…*

A second later she was leaning dangerously forward. An ancient travelling coach had stopped halfway up the hill and an enormous old woman was struggling out. She was too far away for Peony to hear what she was saying, but she was shaking her fist and stamping her feet. For a couple of minutes she stood and argued with the driver; he kept shrugging and pointing at his pocket. Then there was a puff of smoke and his horse turned pink. The driver gave a terrified scream and the horse set off back down the hill at a gallop, the coach bumping and rattling behind.

"Goodness!" Peony stared in astonishment as the old woman rubbed her hands together in glee. "Who is she?"

"That's the Hag," said a voice in her ear, and Peony all but fell out of the tree in surprise. The palace cat was sitting on a branch above her head, cleaning his whiskers. "And you can be sure that she's up to no good. You need to watch her."

Peony stared at the cat. "Did … did you just TALK to me?"

"Well, it certainly wasn't the pigeon. Stupid things, pigeons." Basil extended a paw, studied it, then began to clean between his toes. "Name's Basil, by the way. How do you do?"

"I … I'm very well, thank you." Peony was trying hard not to keep staring. "Erm … can I ask you something?"

Basil blinked his large yellow eyes. "I expect you want to know why I haven't spoken to you before." When Peony nodded, he went on, "I didn't need to. That's the answer. But if the Hag's creeping round there's going to be trouble, and I prefer a quiet life. Wickedness sours the milk." He finished grooming his toes, gave them an admiring glance and sat up. "What's she doing now?"

Peony turned and looked down. The Hag, moving surprisingly fast for such a big woman, had scuttled into the bushes that bordered the wide driveway. Now she was zigzagging to and fro, gradually getting closer to the palace.

"Is she a witch?" Peony asked.

"She's a bad fairy," Basil told her. "I don't suppose you happen to know if your parents invited her to the christening?"

Peony rubbed her nose thoughtfully. "I don't

think so. They did invite three Fairy Godmothers – I heard them talking about it."

"Oh dear." Basil shook his head. "That's unfortunate. Don't your parents know about these things? You must ALWAYS invite all the fairies who live in or near your kingdom, or the ones who are left out get terribly angry and cause no end of problems." He paused. "The Hag will know the Fairy Godmothers have been invited. She's clever, as well as evil. And she also knows they're old. Very old. And – if you don't mind my mentioning it – very underused."

"Underused?" Peony looked blank.

"Fairies have magic powers, but their powers fade away if they don't have the chance to practise. The Hag, on the other hand…" The cat rolled his eyes. "She'll have been keeping her spells brewing, and they'll have grown stronger and stronger."

"So what should we do? Should I tell Father?"

Peony started to wriggle along her branch.

"Certainly not!" The cat's whiskers bristled. "Without wishing to be rude, Princess, that would be a disaster."

"Oh." Peony rubbed her nose again. "I rather expected that you'd say that."

The cat gave her a sideways look. "So – it seems that it's up to you."

"Me? Just me? Aren't you going to help?" Peony asked.

Basil considered the question. "Perhaps. I do prefer good to evil. And the Fairy Godmothers have always paid me well." He stood up on the branch and stretched. "You keep watch from here for a while. I'll go and see what's happening inside the palace." And with a twitch of his whiskers he was gone.

Peony turned to see where the Hag had got to. She was in a clump of ornamental grass at the top of the driveway, and was fishing in her pockets.

That's a very strange dress, was Peony's first thought. Her second was, *Oh my goodness! What IS she doing? Why is she pulling that string out of her pockets? And look at all those carriages! The first guests are arriving already!*

Chapter Fifteen

PEONY WAS RIGHT. She leant back against a branch and watched as carriages, coaches, horse-drawn traps and single riders made their way up the hill. All the important, grand and wealthy inhabitants of the kingdom had been invited to the christening breakfast and, as invitations to the palace were few and far between, they had all accepted. On and on they came as the sun rose higher and higher. They were dressed in their finest clothes; Peony glanced down at her torn and grubby dress as the last carriage trundled towards her. "I'll definitely have to clean up a bit

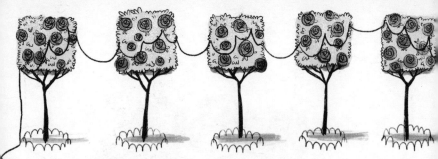

if I'm going to go to the party. Hello! Those must be the Fairy Godmothers."

The Fairy Godmothers were wearing their summery dresses, and their wings glittered in the sunshine. As they swept towards the palace the prime minister came out to greet them; Peony ducked down among the branches, although there was no way that Skeldith could see her. Cautiously peering out again, she noticed the Hag was no longer hiding in the grass. She had left a tangle of string behind her, but that was all.

"Where can she be?" Peony wondered. Scanning the drive and the gardens, she climbed even higher and looked again. From her new viewpoint she eventually spotted the Hag hiding in the tangle of roses under her bedroom window. The fairy was

bending down, tying
string to the rosebushes.

"That's strange," Peony
murmured. "How did she get there without
anyone noticing? Why haven't the guards stopped
her?"

"She's a fairy, remember." Basil was back,
strolling along the branch beneath her. "She can
fade into the background, so nobody can see her
unless they're looking very carefully."

"Oh! She's off!" Peony reported. "She's going
round the other side … and you're right. She
went straight past the guards at the front door and
they didn't notice her at all." She shook her head
in wonder.

Basil shrugged. "That's fairies for you. Don't you want to know what's going on in the banqueting hall?"

"Of course I do." Peony turned to look at him. "Has the christening started yet?"

"There's a lot of chitter-chatter." The cat sniffed. "Your father has a remarkably splendid throne. Your mother looked a little peevish when she saw it. All the guests have arrived, by the way. They've closed the doors."

Peony leant forward. "Did you see my baby brother? Is he all right?"

"He's being looked after by that Beef woman." Basil sounded less than enthusiastic.

The princess sighed. "I can't help wondering – what if the bad fairy tries to hurt him?"

The cat jumped up beside her, and put a furry paw on her hand. "We must make sure that doesn't happen."

"Look!" Peony pointed. "She's moving again …

and she's still holding loads of string. What IS she doing?"

"Nothing good," Basil said. "You can be sure of—"

He was interrupted by the sound of trumpets. There was a long fanfare, a moment's pause, and then another fanfare.

"That'll be Father arriving in the royal banqueting hall." Peony looked down at the palace roof. "It feels odd to think the christening's going on without me being there."

Basil wasn't listening. His eyes had narrowed and he was watching the Hag with intense concentration. "She's circling the palace," he said. "That's bad … very bad."

Peony had already begun to scramble down the tree. "I have to find out what's going on," she said. "I absolutely can't stay here any longer."

The cat didn't move. He had noticed something Peony had not: the bundles of string that the Hag was leaving behind her were beginning to glow a faint green. "Magic," he said to himself. "Bad magic…"

Several branches below, Peony looked up. "Aren't you coming?" she asked.

Basil was still staring. "Princess," he said, "I think you ought to see this." He began to hiss. Peony, hearing the urgency in his voice, swung herself back up the tree to join him – and gasped.

The Hag had made a complete circle of the building and now she was dancing up and down waving her arms. **"Wooooooo!"** she chanted. **"Woooooooo! Wooooooooo!"**

A faint green mist began to rise, a mist that quickly thickened into a dense fog that swirled and twirled until it had the look of a green hedge surrounding the palace. The fog drifted steadily closer and closer to the walls, and Peony saw first one and then another guard collapse in a snoring heap on the palace steps. The captain of the

guard, who was tall enough to see over the top of the swirling green, opened his mouth to call for help, but the Hag flicked her fingers and a tendril of mist twisted round his head. His eyes closed and he sank to the ground. In another moment not one guard was left standing.

"Oh my goodness." Peony was breathless with astonishment. "Oh my goodness gracious me!"

"Not much goodness about it," the cat said.

"That'll gradually seep in through the doors and windows, and send them all to sleep."

"Wooooooo! Wooooooooo!" The Hag was still dancing, her voice growing shriller and shriller. "That'll teach them to forget me! Tee hee hee hee! **Sleeping twine, sleeping twine … all asleep, that baby's mine!"**

Peony was very pale. "I was right: she wants the baby! We've got to do something – we've got to save him!"

"Of course," Basil said. "But what about the fog? You saw how quickly those guards went to sleep."

"Mmmmm…" Peony was thinking as hard as she could. "What if I could get higher than the fog? So I don't breathe it in?"

"Above it?" Basil considered this idea. "But how could you? You'd need to be quite remarkably tall – much taller than the guards."

"Exactly!" Peony's eyes were shining. "Mr Wells – he's taller than everyone! I could ride on his shoulders and the fog wouldn't come near me. And guess what?" She was quivering with excitement. "I've had another idea! The musicians' gallery … the gallery above the hall. You can see everything from there. I used to spy on the royal feasts! And there's a window… How long have I got before everyone's asleep?"

"How long?" The cat blinked. "I couldn't say … but the fog's moving."

He was right. The fog was clearing at the back of the palace and growing thicker and thicker at the front, as the Hag beckoned it towards her with a long bony finger. Alternately cackling and chanting, she pointed at the door. **"Wooooooo! One, two, three, four, open wide the royal door!"**

The huge golden door swung open and the fog began to ooze inside. "Right. Here I go," said Peony, and she scrambled down the tree. Next minute she was running through the cherry trees towards the back of the palace and the window of the dungeon.

She hurled the rope over the empty window frame before climbing up to knot it round the centre bar. Then she called down. "Mr Wells? I need your help! I really, really do – please help me. PLEASE!"

Chapter Sixteen

Down in the dungeon Horrington Wells woke
with a start. For a second he thought he was
dreaming, but then he was wide awake and on his
feet. Grabbing the sheet rope he began to climb,
and Lionel Longbeard, peering out from under
his blanket and rubbing his eyes, was just in time
to see the jester's long legs disappearing through
the window. The rope was left hanging; after a
moment the dwarf, with much puffing, followed
his friend. He found him with a bright-eyed Peony.

"Can you see that horrid green fog creeping
round the walls? That's magic! A bad fairy called

the Hag made a spell with sleeping twine, and it sends you to sleep as soon as you breathe it in – and the Hag wants to steal my brother – so I need to get into the palace!" Peony stopped for breath. "I'm going to climb into the banqueting hall. There's a little window at the back that's always open – but I need to stand on your shoulders so I can reach it. It's the window in the musicians' gallery; nobody'll see me."

Horrington bowed deeply. "Your wish is my command, Princess."

Lionel pulled at his sleeve. "But the king, man! What about the king?"

The jester shrugged. "The child needs help."

"Thank you!" Peony beamed at him. She untied the rope and slung it over her arm. "Can we go right now?"

"Climb on my shoulders." Horrington glanced towards the heavy green mist.

Peony caught his gaze and nodded. "Isn't it

horrid? But we'll be above it. It's wonderful you're so tall." Another thought came to her. "Can we sneak to the side of the palace and see what the Hag's up to?"

"One moment." The dwarf coughed. "Might I make a suggestion? While you make your way into the palace, Princess, I could attempt to stop this magic at its source."

Peony blinked. "I'm sorry … I'm not sure what you mean."

"He means the sleeping twine." Basil had appeared beside them.

"Sleeping twine," Lionel said thoughtfully. "I've read about that kind of spell. When a knot is loosened the magic grows less. Two knots untied, and the magic stops."

Peony looked at him with awe. "Oh, Mr Longbeard! You have the WIDEST mind. When all this is over I'm going to come to your library every single day."

"You'll be welcome." Lionel gave a nod and followed Basil to the nearest tangle of twine. "Ah," he said as he sat down beside it. "A cunning twist … but it can be undone with care and thought."

As the dwarf set to work, Horrington, with Peony on his shoulders, tiptoed to the corner of the palace and peered cautiously round. His head and shoulders were high above the magic mist and he and the princess had no trouble spotting the Hag. She was running up to the fog, then falling back and stamping her feet in fury.

"What's she doing?" Peony whispered. "It's her magic. Why doesn't she just walk through it?"

"Woooooo!" the Hag shrieked. **"Woooooo! Woooooo! WOOOOOO!"**

She made another run at the green barrier, and this time she vanished – but a moment later she reappeared, coughing and spluttering and wiping her streaming eyes. "Too much deadly nightshade. I knew it! I knew it! Should've added a frog. Or a couple of newts…" Still muttering, she pulled a bent wand from her pocket and waved it in front of her. **"Woooooo, woooooo – let me through!"**

The fog shivered and drew back just enough to offer a narrow pathway leading to the palace door.

"Wider! Wider! WOOOOOOO!" The Hag was the colour of a beetroot, but the fog had done as much as it was prepared to do. It turned a sulky grey and the pathway turned into a tunnel.

"Oh POOO!" the Hag said, and she began to squeeze her way towards the palace.

Horrington shook his head. "No time to waste." He strode back, Peony giving him directions, until they were standing under a small, high window. Horrington, looking up at it, measured the distance with his eye. "Hmmm," he said doubtfully.

"If you don't mind me standing on your shoulders again, Mr Wells, I can catch hold of the ledge," Peony said.

The jester nodded, and when Peony was standing up, one hand on the wall, he saw she was right: the window was just within her reach. "Nearly there!" she said, and she stretched up to get a fingerhold. Horrington stood on tiptoe and Peony gave a squeak of excitement. "That's it!" Her feet kicked wildly. "Here … I … go!" And she was gone.

In no time at all she was looking out at him.

"I've just thought of something," she whispered. "I've escaped *out* of the palace twice in the last two days – and now I'm breaking *in*! Isn't that extraordinary? Would you mind waiting here? I'll be back soon!" And she vanished again, only to reappear with the end of the sheet rope in her hand. "Could you hold on to this?"

"Princess!" Horrington called. "Don't do anything risky—"

But Peony was out of earshot.

Chapter Seventeen

THE MUSICIANS' GALLERY above the royal banqueting
hall was never used. King Thoroughgood had
declared that music gave him indigestion, and
nobody official had been up there in years. Only
Peony's footprints could be seen in the thick dust,
and she had to hold her nose to keep herself from
sneezing.

She crept to the front and looked down. Her
father was sitting immediately below her so she
could see the top of his head, and her sisters and
mother were beside him, facing the crowds
of guests.

There's no sign of the fog yet, Peony thought, *but when Father sees people falling asleep all over the place he'll know something's wrong.*

The baby's cradle was placed in the centre of the hall, and as Peony stifled yet another sneeze the three Fairy Godmothers wafted their way forward to stand beside it. Miss Beef drew back the lace coverlet so little Prince Vicenzo could be seen. His red hair flamed on the pillow, and his

cheeks were very pink as he gazed at the fairies with round blue eyes.

Up above, Peony smiled. "Darling baby," she breathed.

"Your Majesties! We thank you for your hospitality," Fairy Geraldine announced, and she sank into a deep curtsy.

King Thoroughgood stood up. "We welcome you, and look forward to your gifts."

Fairy Jacqueline raised her eyebrows at Fairy Geraldine. "Gifts? Did we mention gifts?"

The king sat down again.

"Shh, Jacqueline dear," Fairy Josephine said. "Your Majesty, we are delighted to celebrate the birth of your son. I fear our skills are a little rusty, due to lack of use—" She fixed the king with a meaningful gaze— "but we have done our best. I had hoped to bring the gift of endless gold, but alas! It was beyond me. Instead I have brought the gift of laughter." She waved a hand over the cradle

and the baby began to gurgle happily. Peony
was unable to see her father's reaction, but Fairy
Josephine's face made her suspect he was not
grateful.

Poor fairy, Peony thought, and she glanced over
the heads of the guests to the double doors at the
back of the hall. At first she wondered if she was
imagining the wisps of mist floating through,
but when the guests at the furthest table began
to yawn she knew the magic had begun to work.
She tiptoed over to the window and peered out.
Horrington was standing
firm, the end of the rope
in his hands.

"And what, pray, is the meaning of this?"

Peony swung round. The king was angry – very angry – but he was not looking at her. Raised up above the queen and his daughters, he was staring down at the tables crammed with guests … guests who were drooping over their plates or leaning back in their chairs with their eyes closed. Queen Dilys had collapsed on her throne and Peony's six sisters had their heads in their hands, and the baby had stopped gurgling and was fast asleep. Miss Beef had sunk down on the floor

in a mound of black velvet and was snoring loudly. The front row was yawning dreadfully, and so were the three Fairy Godmothers; Fairy Jacqueline and Fairy Josephine were propped up by a pillar, and Fairy Geraldine was supporting herself on a spindly chair. Moments later they too were snoring.

"Oh no!" Peony had never expected the magic to move so fast. She grabbed her end of the rope, scrambled over the edge of the gallery and took a deep breath. *Mustn't breathe in any mist*, she told herself as she slid down.

Her father opened and closed his mouth like an enormous goldfish. His throne lifted him a little way above the fog so the magic had not had its full effect; of all the many people in the hall, he was the only one not asleep.

She tucked the baby under one arm, seized the rope, and began to climb. Once she had managed to struggle over the gallery rail, holding the baby

tightly, she let out her breath
with a huge *phew*.

"I'm so sorry, Father,"
she called, "But I've
absolutely got to
save Vicenzo
from the Hag.
I'll come back
and get you as
soon as he's safe."

Then, running to the window, she leant out.
"Mr Wells! Mr Wells! Could you look after the
baby? The Hag's coming!"

There was no time for Horrington to object;
Peony was already lowering the little prince.
Vicenzo opened his eyes and chuckled as he
settled himself comfortably in Horrington's arms.
"Urgle urgle!"

"There!" Peony said. "He likes you! I'll be back
just as soon as I know Father and Mother haven't

been turned into frogs or bats."

"Princess!" It was Lionel Longbeard, running to Horrington's side. "Princess – we've undone one bundle of sleeping twine, but we need more time for the second. The knots are very tight. The cat is at work right now and we can do it – but we must have another few minutes."

Peony nodded. "I'll do what I can. Promise."

As Peony hurried back, she could almost have believed the banqueting hall was empty. Except for the sounds of snoring, and the occasional snort, the silence was unbroken. Moving to the side of the gallery she caught sight of her father. Slumped on his throne, his eyes looked up at her and she saw that for the first time in his life he was asking for help.

"Oh, Father—" Peony began, but she was interrupted by a loud bang as the double doors crashed open and the Hag burst in, cackling gleefully. "HA! HA HA HA HA HA! Here I am, my royal friends! Me – the Hag of Scrabster's Hump! The one you forgot to ask to your party!"

Chapter Eighteen

STORMING UP TO THE KING, the Hag snapped her bony fingers under his nose. "You can hear me and see me, can't you, Thoroughgood – and if ever a king had a foolish name, it's you! I'm here to make you sorry – oh, so very, very sorry!"

Dancing up and down, she stuck out her tongue at the three sleeping Fairy Godmothers. "Look! They can't help you – they're much too old and feeble. Yah! Bah! Silly old bags. And guess what I'm going to do with your little bubsy wubsy?" The Hag let out a screech of delight as the king began to tremble, and Peony leant forward, holding her breath. "I'm going to take your precious little son, and you'll never, ever, ever see him again!" And she moved towards the cradle.

"No! She mustn't see it's empty – she'll go mad." Peony searched frantically in her pockets and brought out a handful of cherry stones. "YES!" Balancing one on the gallery rail, she flicked it at the Hag. It hit the fairy right on the end of her nose; she jumped and swore violently before twisting to see where it had come from. Peony ducked down and crawled to the other side of the gallery. The Hag, seeing nothing, swore again. As soon as her back was turned, Peony flicked another cherry stone. It hit a wine glass with a loud *ping!* and the glass shattered.

"Who did that?" the Hag snapped, and she peered angrily at the queen and Peony's sisters. "Was it one of you?" She swung round to the guests, collapsed among the plates and silver and flowers. Not one of them was moving, and she gave a suspicious grunt. "Something strange is going on." She paused, and her beady little eyes gleamed. "Aha! Of course." She swept up to the Fairy Godmothers, and stopped with her face inches away from Fairy Geraldine's. "Well, well, well … so it's not you after all. You're snoring too loudly."

Peony fired another cherry stone. It hit the prime minister on the ear and he stirred a little. "Go 'way," he mumbled. "Nasty fly…"

The Hag went purple. "NO! Someone spoke! Is my magic fading? It's not possible!" She pulled out her wand and waved it wildly above her head. **"Sleeping twine, sleeping twine… Go to sleep. That baby's MINE!"** and she rushed at the cradle.

"STOP!" Peony jumped to her feet. "Stop! The baby's gone. I took him away. You can't have him!"

"Aaaaaaaaaaaaaaaaaaaaaaagh!" The Hag's scream echoed round and round the banqueting hall. She glared up at Peony, her face twitching with fury. "I don't know who you are," she hissed, "but I'm going to make sure you never cross me again, you horrid little worm … because I'm going to turn you into a FROG!" Swelling with anger and frustration she pointed her wand. Green and purple sparks flew into the air as she began to chant—

And it was at that precise moment that Lionel Longbeard and Basil the cat, frantically working in the midst of the rosebushes, undid the final knot on the second bundle of twine. The green fog vanished … and the Hag's snakeskin dress

split from top to bottom, revealing a grubby yellow vest and patched spotty knickers.

"Aaaaaaaaaaaaaaaaaaaaaaaagh!" Her scream was even more piercing than before. She dropped her wand and ran for the doors, still screaming, and fought her way out – straight into the arms of the guards. "AAAAAAAAAGH!" Her legs kicking wildly, she was carried away to the dungeons. Behind her there was a rustling and a creaking, a murmuring and a stretching as the guests sat up and rubbed their bleary eyes.

"Oh! The spell's wearing off." Peony clapped her hands in delight. Queen Dilys shook herself and looked up. She caught sight of Peony, dusty, scratched, smeared with cherry juice and wearing something so torn and dirty it was unrecognisable.

"Peony? Peony! You NAUGHTY girl. What do you think you're doing?" She looked over at the cradle. "Oh me! Oh my! The BABY – someone's stolen my baby! Call the guards! Call the guards – Thoroughgood! DO something!" And she dissolved into floods of hysterical tears.

The guests, aware that something very extraordinary was happening, stared as the king slowly rose to his feet. He took no notice of his wife's demands. Instead he turned and faced Peony.

"Peony," he said, "I believe I saw you save your brother. Where is he now?"

Peony was very pale, but she managed to smile. "Vicenzo's outside, Father. You can stop crying, Mother. He's quite safe."

"But Peony … Peony! Whatever have you been doing?" her mother wailed.

Miss Beef, yawning hugely, heaved herself up from the floor and came bustling forward.

"Let me take care of this, Your Majesties. Princess Peony's shocking behaviour will be punished most severely—"

"No," said the king. "No. There will be no punishment."

"Oh yes there will." Miss Beef shook her finger at the musicians' gallery. "This is yet another example of Peony's rebellious nature! I INSIST that she receives the punishment she deserves!"

"And I," said King Thoroughgood, "insist that you, Miss Beef, leave my employment right now this minute."

The governess gawped at him and the six princesses froze in their seats.

"Did you hear me, Miss Beef?" The king's eyes flashed. "You're dismissed. Now go!"

Speechless with indignation, the governess stalked away between the tables. Her face was scarlet, but she held her head high and as she left she slammed the doors behind her with a mighty crash.

King Thoroughgood looked up at Peony. "Peony, my child – today you have done something extraordinarily brave. You saved your brother, Prince Vicenzo. Won't you come down?"

"I can't," Peony said, and her voice was trembling. "The Hag's magic worked. I … I've got frog's feet." She stumbled her way to the small spiral staircase linking the musicians' gallery to

the hall and stood there shivering ... and there
was a universal gasp.

Her feet were webbed and green.

Chapter Nineteen

EVERYONE IN THE BANQUETING hall had something to say, and Queen Dilys started crying even louder than before.

"Silence!" King Thoroughgood held up his hand. "Silence!" As the noise died away, he took off his crown. "It seems to me that I have – erm." An expression of acute self-consciousness crossed his face and he coughed. "*Ahem*. This is difficult for me to say … but it must be said. I have made mistakes. *Ahem*. And because of my … erm … mistakes, my precious daughter is the victim of an evil spell … and she needs help. So, I apologise.

And if anyone – anyone!" His voice shook, but he pulled himself together and went on, "If anyone can help her, I will be eternally grateful."

"Well, well, well." It was Fairy Jacqueline, and her eyes were sparkling. "I never thought this day would come. A request from the King of Grating? But of course we'll help! We're your Fairy Godmothers! We only needed to be asked, you know. Geraldine, dear, and Josephine – three wands are always better than one. Are you ready? Good. One … two … three … go!"

This time the sparks were gold and silver, and for several seconds the banqueting hall was filled with the sound of singing birds and tinkling bells. Rose petals floated over the floor, multicoloured ribbons streamed from the walls and thousands of tiny stars twinkled on the ceiling.

"A little over-the-top, my dears," Fairy Jacqueline remarked as she put down her wand. "Still – we do appear to have had the desired effect. The frog feet have gone."

She was right. A delighted Peony was hurrying down the spiral staircase – but she was only halfway down when the double doors opened and the fascinated guests saw the strange figures of Lionel Longbeard and Horrington Wells framed in the doorway.

Horrington was holding Prince Vicenzo in his arms; Lionel was looking exceedingly nervous.

Peony's eyes shone. "Come in! Come in!"

As they hesitated she ran to meet them, and led them towards her father and mother. "Father, Mother – Mr Wells and Mr Longbeard helped me save Vicenzo. I couldn't have done it without them."

The queen, forgetting all royal etiquette, snatched the baby from Horrington's arms. "If you helped save my baby, you're a truly wonderful man," she said as she covered Vicenzo's face with kisses.

"He is wonderful," Peony said, "and so is Mr Longbeard."

Horrington bowed very low. "We saw the Hag being taken away, Your Majesties, so we thought we should return the little princeling." He bowed again. "Pray excuse our intrusion."

"Intrusion?" Peony shook her head. "How could it be an intrusion? Father, Father … can I ask you something?"

The king didn't answer immediately. He was looking puzzled. "Peony, do I know Mr Wells and Mr Longbeard? I seem to recognise them…"

"Of course you do!" Peony put her hand on her father's sleeve. "You put them in the dungeon! But do you know what, Father? Mr Longbeard knew all about magic, because he's read about it in his library – and so he knew just what to do! And I could never have escaped without Mr Wells – and please, please, PLEASE, dearest Father – please will you say they're free for ever?"

There was a long pause, and then the king picked up his crown and looked at Peony. "I think I have learnt a great deal today," he said. "And it seems I have much more to learn."

Peony leant towards him. "Me too, Father. I really, REALLY need to widen my mind, and if you'll let me go to the library I'm sure I can do it … and I'll tell you something. That giant has to go. He isn't looking after the books properly.

Mr Longbeard has to come back, and I think Mr Wells might like to help him and Miss Denzil. So can they both be free? PLEASE?"

The king placed the crown on his head and sat down on his throne. "I, Thoroughgood, King of Grating, wish to express my profound thanks to Mr Wells and his companion, Mr Longbeard. And in recognition of their services to myself and my family, I hereby grant them the freedom of the kingdom, for ever and for always."

Horrington Wells stepped forward and bowed. "Thank you, Your Majesty."

Lionel Longbeard coughed. "Indeed. That is to say … I agree."

"And they can go back to the library?" Peony insisted.

"They may, of course, return to the library." The king paused. "I shall visit it myself."

Peony beamed. "We'll go together, Father. And we'll take Vicenzo. Miss Denzil will find him loads

of lovely storybooks,

won't she, Mr Longbeard?"

The dwarf nodded. "Miss

Denzil will be delighted to help. As will I. And if

my friend Horrington is willing to join us—"

"Which I am," Horrington put in.

"—then I can assure all here of the warmest

of welcomes." Lionel took off his spectacles and

waved them in the air.

"HIP HIP HOORAY!" Peony led the cheering, but stopped halfway through. "Now I come to think of it, Father, there's one more thing. There's a man in the dungeons who stole a cheese—"

Fairy Jacqueline bent to whisper in her ear. "Peony, dear … enough. Let your father consider these things in his own time. He will."

"Oh…" Peony blushed. "I see what you mean. I'm not being tactful, am I?" She looked hopefully at the fairy. "Will you be staying?" She turned to the king. "Wouldn't that be a good idea, Father? If the Fairy Godmothers stayed here?"

Her father looked appalled, then took a deep breath. "*Ahem*. I don't think that will be necessary, although I'm truly grateful to all the Fairy Godmothers for their help today. And I'll most certainly call if…" He stopped to correct himself. "I mean, *when* I need them."

Fairy Jacqueline gave him her most gracious smile. "I look forward to that moment, Your Majesty."

Fairy Josephine dropped a deep curtsy. "We all do." Peony's sisters were staring at her in astonishment, and the fairy looked at them thoughtfully. "There are so many things we could help you with…"

"Josephine!" Fairy Jacqueline whisked her hastily away as the king stepped forward, smiling at the assembled guests.

"Friends! Dear friends, and my very dear family – what a day this has been! And now it's time for us to celebrate. We'll celebrate the bravery of my daughter Peony and the return of my son … and we must not forget that we have a wonderful christening party to enjoy!"

As the cheers rang out, Fairy Geraldine tiptoed up to Peony. "What's your favourite colour?" she whispered.

Peony needed no time to think. "Cherry red!"

Fairy Geraldine waved her wand … and Peony was wearing the prettiest dress she had ever seen,

let alone owned. "Goodness," she said. "Thank you so, SO much!" Then she saw her sisters' faces. "Oh…" And she whispered in Fairy Geraldine's ear.

"Done!" said the fairy, and Peony's six sisters were wearing dresses in blues and greens and yellows, with a scattering of daisies round the hems. Nobody was rude enough to suggest the flowers looked just a little wilted.

"One more thing," Fairy Josephine said, and she swept down to where the Hag's wand lay abandoned on the floor. Picking it up, she snapped it in half. "There! Without her wand, she won't have any magic powers. In a year or so, when she's had time to consider, we'll visit her."

Fairy Geraldine beamed. "We could teach her to knit!"

Fairy Jacqueline nodded. "Or perhaps to sew. That dress was a disgrace …"

"We'll think about it, my dears," said Fairy Josephine. "But now it's time for a party!"

All the guests agreed it was the most wonderful party they had ever been to. They stayed and stayed … and the king and queen were gracious to everyone. The servants were thanked and promised time off and extra pay. The cake was a huge success, and Skeldith, who was watching anxiously to make sure all went smoothly, was able to heave a huge sigh of relief. Nobody was forgotten … except…

Towards the end of the party, Peony went to find her parents. "Mother, Father … may I be excused? There's someone else I need to thank."

"Why aren't they here?" her mother asked.

Peony shook her head. "He's not very keen on parties. But maybe I could take him some of those little fishy sandwiches."

"Take whatever you like," the king said. "And Peony! I have a special favour to ask."

"A favour?" Peony looked at her father in surprise.

"There's just one thing missing from this splendid

feast: a cherry pie. Nobody makes cherry pies like you do, Peony. Would you consider popping down to the palace kitchen sometime tomorrow and making one? For me?"

Peony beamed. "I'd absolutely love to!" And she hugged her father and blew kisses to her mother as she ran out of the royal banqueting hall.

She found Basil curled up on her bed.

"Basil!" she said, and she picked him up and held him to her heart. "Thank you for everything! Thank you so, SO much! I'm the happiest girl in the whole wide world!"

Basil stretched out a paw and inspected his toes. "When you go to the library," he said, "you'll find the best stories all end, 'And the princess lived Happily Ever After...'"

He began to purr.

THE END

Also by Vivian French

ALFIE ONION is setting out
on a great adventure. His brother
Magnifico is off to make the
family's fortune ... and Alfie's
carrying his luggage! But it turns
out Magnifico hates adventures
and Alfie has to save the day –
with a little help from his loyal
dog, a talking horse, two mice and
some meddling magpies.

For older readers
TALES FROM THE FIVE KINGDOMS

"24-carat gold. I forgot reading
could be this much fun!"
Philip Ardagh

"Hilarious adventures with
wicked witches, trolls, bats and
fairy-tale magic." *Books for Keeps*

"Delightfully witty and exciting."
Independent on Sunday

"Fabulous." *Daily Telegraph*

"So good, I was up all night
reading. But don't tell my mum!"
Grace, aged 11½

Vivian French

lives in Edinburgh, and writes in a messy workroom
stuffed full of fairy tales and folk tales — the stories she
loves best. She's brilliant at retelling classic tales, as she
did for *The Most Wonderful Thing in the World*, and has
created worlds of her own in *The Adventures of Alfie Onion*
and the Tales From the Five Kingdoms series. Vivian
teaches at Edinburgh College of Art and can be seen
at festivals all over the country. She is one of the most
borrowed children's authors in UK libraries, and in 2016
was awarded the MBE for services to literature, literacy,
illustration and the arts.

Marta Kissi

is an exciting new talent in the world of children's book
illustration. Originally from Warsaw, she came to Britain
to study Illustration and Animation at Kingston
University, and then Art and Design at the Royal College
of Art. Her favourite part of being an illustrator is bringing
stories to life by designing charming characters and the
wonderful worlds they live in. Marta shares a studio in
London with her boyfriend and their pet plant Trevor.